Ocean Deep

Yan Nascimbene

Creative Editions

To Suzi

Published in 1999 by Creative Editions 123 South Broad Street, Mankato, MN 56001 USA *Creative Editions* is an imprint of The Creative Company Designed by Rita Marshall Printed in Italy. Library of Congress Cataloging-in-Publication Data Nascimbene, Yan. Ocean deep / written and illustrated by Yan Nascimbene. ISBN 1-56846-161-5 [1. Switzerland~Fiction. 2. Boarding schools~Fiction. 3. Schools~Fiction.] I. Title. PZ7.N16550g 1999 [Fic]~dc21 98-50011 5 4 3 2 1 First Edition

L Ú C I A

PUSHES BACK THE SHEET AND SITS UP. She walks past the row of beds to the end of the dormitory. Her elongated shadow slides over the children's sleeping faces, unsettling the pale blue glow of the moon. Lúcia stands by the window; she looks at the stars. She watches them twinkling above the black mountain ridge; at the same instant her parents might be watching the stars over the ocean far away.

A girl murmurs a few unintelligible words in her sleep. Lúcia stands still, her head tilted to the sky. The linoleum floor is cold under her feet. The dawn erases the stars one by one, then the night.

Lúcia's parents are on vacation, sailing on a large ship through the West Indies, far from her home in São Paulo, far from Madame Amédroz's Châlet les Gentianes, a boarding

house for children in the Swiss Alps where she is to stay until summer's end.

A new morning. A new day. And again the night. Day after day, night after night.

MADAME AMÉDROZ HANDS OUT A CHEESE SANDWICH, an orange, a small carton of juice and a bar of chocolate to each child. Lúcia stuffs the food in her backpack, she lays her sweater on top and latches the canvas flap.

The children walk in a line along the narrow streets. Deep in the heart of the valley the village is still immersed in cool blue shade, yet high above the sunlight flows quickly down the mountainside. Madame Amédroz leads the march. Her assistant, Monsieur Kobler, walks last. Lúcia trips over an empty soda can; she kicks it. Placing a secret bet, she kicks it over and over as she walks: *If I can roll it all the way to the fountain I'll be back home in São Paulo really, really soon.*

The air smells of hay and mud, it smells of cows.

Past the fountain they take a road uphill. A few hairpin curves. The village below, a fragile miniature, disappears behind a clump of birch trees. The road narrows down to a dirt path, it winds through a pine forest, dark and damp. Sweet scents of moss, fern, bark.

Walking out of the woods, the children are blinded by the sun, which now spreads all over the pasture. They follow a stream to a gently sloped plateau. Distant cowbells mix with the roar of water.

LÚCIA LAYS DOWN HER BACKPACK. As she sits, grasshoppers scatter about. Some children build a dam across the stream. They pile up rocks, filling the gaps with smaller stones and gravel.

Lúcia gazes at the snow-covered mountain peaks. She turns to the lower end of the valley which, in a hazy blur, dissolves into the plain. She looks at the hillside dotted with flowers. Lying down on her stomach

she examines the flowers. She picks the ones around her, then the ones further away. Lúcia remembers gathering wildflowers with her mother. Searching for different kinds, she walks to the end of the plateau, past a rocky promontory. As the children's laughter and shrieking fade, the cowbells' jingle draws near.

A single cloud, fluffy and white, floats by. A bee flies near and vanishes.

Sharp pounding suddenly breaks the afternoon quiet.

Someone is hammering. Lúcia takes a few more steps. As if rising from the ground a barn appears behind the hill. She stops. The hammering stops. Lúcia keeps very still. Halfway between her and the barn, a cow takes a few steps, very slowly, her bell ringing softly. Then the hammering begins again, echoing louder and louder through the valley as she runs back to the plateau.

Lúcia sets the bouquet of flowers next to her backpack and sits, watching the children pile more and more stones across the stream. Her heart is beating loudly, as if the hammering is caught inside her.

AFTER BREAKFAST, if Madame Amédroz has not planned any outing, the children play on the terrace and the gravel yard facing les Gentianes. The parasol casts a pink shadow on the round metal table scattered with wildflowers. One by one Lúcia picks up the flowers and places them between sheets of paper.

Occasionally a car drives by. Lúcia glances at it through the honeysuckle and the chicken-wire fence. Suitcases are stacked on racks. Children look out, smiling, laughing, the wind blowing their hair through open side windows.

Lúcia arranges a purple flower next to an orange one. Leaning back she looks at the Mont Blanc glistening with sunlight; the mountain seems strong and confident. She pulls a crumpled postcard out of her

pocket: Blue and turquoise water, coconut trees, a beach of white sand. She gazes at it for a long time then flips it over. She has read it many times, now she knows it by heart: "Queridinha, it is beautiful here. Papa and I think of you a lot. We are quite busy, but we shall come as soon as we can. I love you. Mamãe."

Long past bedtime Lúcia stares at the postcard propped up on her nightstand. She resists falling asleep: her sleep is often filled with terrifying nightmares.

LÚCIA AND N'GUEMA, A BOY YOUNGER THAN HER, stand by the chicken-wire fence. N'guema has counted eight red cars, Lúcia only two green ones. They would rather keep counting cars and watching the road, which leads to the city, to the airport, and back to their homes, than go on the daily hike.

As the children reach the plateau, marmots whistle to each other, warning of their arrival. The water has risen, creating a small pond where children gather tadpoles and put them in jars. Others keep adding

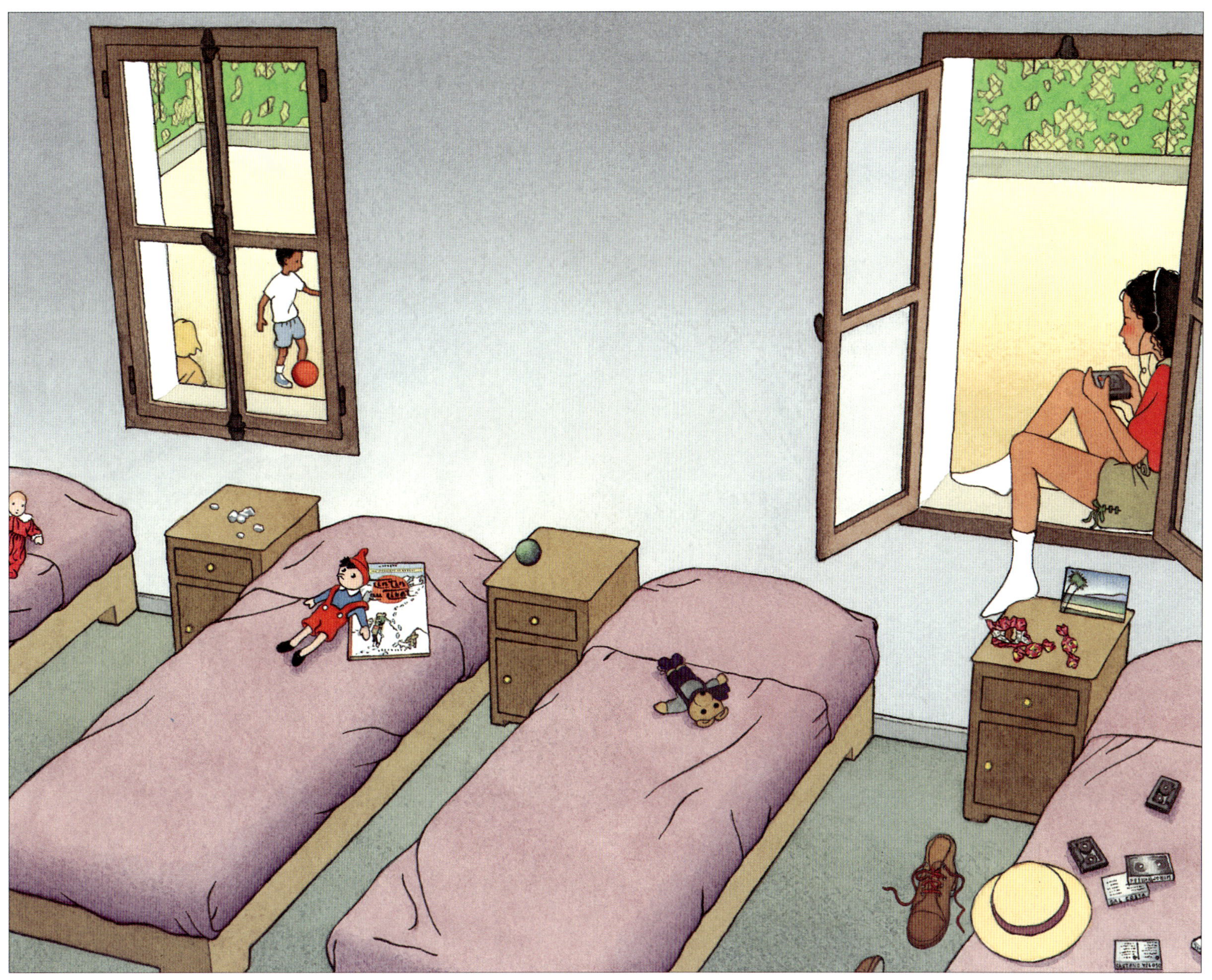

rocks to the dam, trying to prevent the stream from flowing over it. Beyond the gushing of water and the steady hum of a million insects, Lúcia can hear—very faint—the distant hammering.

Glancing right and left, she walks to the end of the plateau. When Madame Amédroz looks up in her direction, Lúcia bends down, picks a flower or two, then, as Madame Amédroz tilts her head back to her knitting, Lúcia hurries away. She climbs the rocks overlooking the plateau. Soon she sees the barn. The hammering reverberates all around her; it is deafening.

THE HAMMERING HAS STOPPED. Now she hears the grinding of a saw. As Lúcia approaches the barn, the grinding stops as well. A man comes out. She stands still. He smiles and bows at her from a distance. "I'm Lúcia, what's your name?" "Aldo," says the man. Lúcia walks up. She crosses the stream over a narrow bridge. "Hello," he says as he crouches by her

and shakes her hand. He is a tall man, his black hair and face are covered with sawdust. An infinite kindness shines from his eyes, which keep smiling even when he isn't.

Looking over his shoulder, Lúcia peeks through the open door of a small cabin next to the barn. "Is this your home?" she asks. She steps inside: A table, a chair, a mattress, it is bare and clean. As her eyes adjust to the dim light, a photograph looms out of the dark: A beach of white sand, the ocean, turquoise and blue glowing more and more intensely. Next to it on the wall is a map: Islands it seems, a lot of lines and numbers. This is where Aldo lives, all spring, all summer with six cows and his dog, Bimba. The cows graze freely while he works in the barn."What kind of work?" He won't say. The large door to the barn is kept shut.

As they walk back out, Aldo reaches below the bridge for a metal bucket full of milk and hands it to Lúcia. The milk is creamy, sweet, and ice cold. Drops run down her chin and neck, glistening pearls on her amber skin.

N'guema and two other boys are racing toy cars on a track they have traced through the gravel. Michelle, the little girl from Los Angeles, chases butterflies. Alessandro and Naoual are watching the tadpoles: some have grown hind legs. They add fresh water to the jar. As Lúcia lifts the jar from the stack of books, the tadpoles swim frantically through the mossy pebbles and blades of grass. She then picks up the books lent to her by Madame Amédroz. One of them, *La Flore Alpine*, is a book about wildflowers. It lists their names, all hard to read and impossible to pronounce. One by one Lúcia pulls up the sheets of paper, uncovering the pressed flowers. She has given them better names: Purple hat, Curly, Tiny blue me, Saudosa, Red lips, Estrelinhas, Cotton swab flower. She glues them in a notebook, arranging them according to shape, size, and color.

Lúcia sets one aside—Ocean Deep—and slips it in an envelope addressed to her parents.

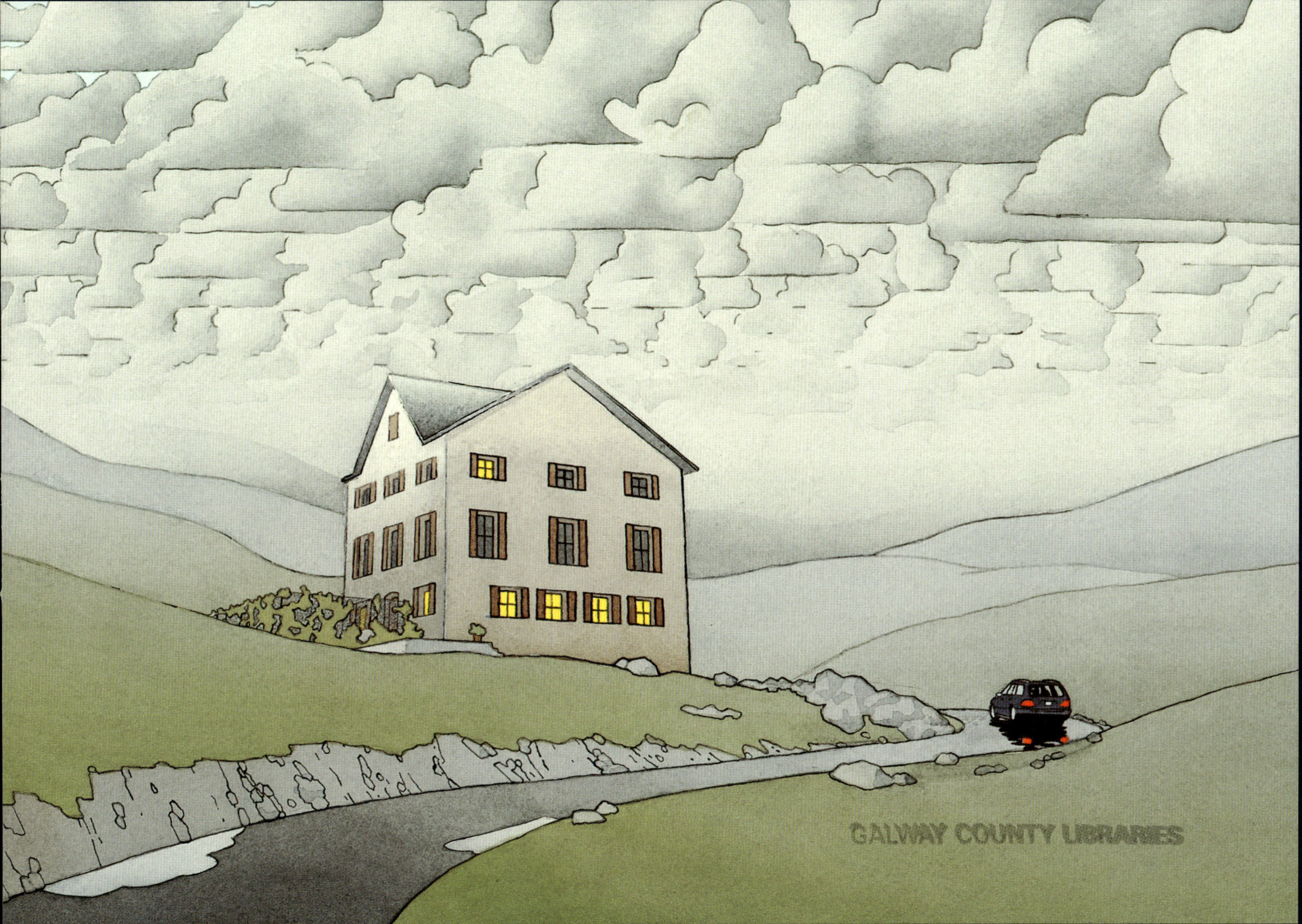

Rainy day
Call it a flower
Tiny blue me
Broken sunset
Batucada
Tomorrow
Doce de leite
Moonlight
Lágrima prateada

Pinky
For N'guema
Hush
Purple hat
Bimba
Tutu
Saudosa
A little pretty
Poof!

MADAME AMÉDROZ WALKS THE CHILDREN TO THE PLATEAU ALMOST EVERY DAY. While some keep strengthening the dam, others play hide-and-seek in the nearby forest or slide down the grassy slope on large slabs of slate. Meanwhile, Lúcia sneaks away to Aldo's cabin. Lúcia and Aldo sit on a wooden bench by the stream, their backs against the warm stone wall. Sometimes his cows come near. Aldo calls them by their names. Stroking their noses gently, he whispers a few kind words in their ears. Other times the cows are nowhere to be seen, Lúcia only hears their distant bells.

She talks about her parents, her home, her far-away country. Then she is quiet. While Aldo walks in and out of the cabin, fixing a lamp, stacking logs, rearranging canned goods on the shelves, Lúcia sits still, looking away.

The air is cool. She shivers from an occasional gust of wind, yet the sun is burning her legs.

Aldo walks to her: "Come, Lúcia." As he leads her to the barn, he pulls a key out of his pocket, unlocks the door and slides it open. The barn looks even bigger inside than it had from the outside. Illuminated by rays of light falling through loose boards, a large sailboat glows like a ghost ship in the semi-darkness. Its white paint is fresh and shiny. The cleats, the cockpit, the boom, the pullies are glossy with varnish, as if coated with glass.

Lúcia strokes the red keel. She climbs up the scaffolding and looks at the high mast. She turns to Aldo. "It's beautiful," she says. "It's a beautiful...boat!" Aldo stands still, he keeps quiet. She laughs, "A boat?! Here?!" Aldo fiddles with his key, he looks away, he doesn't answer.

LÚCIA DREADS THE NIGHT. She dreads the walk upstairs after dinner, but tonight is a special night, August first, a festive night. With some cheese given to her by Aldo, Madame

ALTO
BASSO
FRAGILE

Amédroz has prepared cheese fondue, and she has baked wild berry *tartelettes*. After dinner, instead of the dormitory, she leads the children outside where they are each given a paper lantern. As they walk to the village square, more and more people join in the procession, all holding lanterns on long sticks. The lights dangle in the night as those in Lúcia's garden at home: Strands of colored lightbulbs hang over the table as she eats outside with her parents on summer nights. Lúcia squints: All she sees are lights in the night.

The music is faint; hidden in its beat she distinguishes the distant hammering.

THE TADPOLES HAVE GROWN INTO TINY FROGS. As the children release them in the stream, they hop and swim away, hiding in the shade of large rocks. N'guema sits alone in the grass, downhill from Lúcia. He turns to her, she smiles faintly. Then, as he looks away, she watches him. He looks down, playing with his shoelaces. N'guema reminds her of a friend from school in São Paulo. She wipes her eyes and stands up.

Lúcia hurries to Aldo's house. She knocks. There is no answer. She pushes the door, looks around: He isn't there. Coming back out she walks to the barn, the door has been left ajar. She slides it open a bit more, peeks inside.

A ladder is leaning against the boat, inviting her to climb aboard. The ropes are gathered on the wooden deck in neat spirals. Facing the helm the compass casts a green glare. Lúcia steps down into the hull. Lit by two brass bracket lamps, the map which she had seen pinned inside Aldo's cabin lays unfolded on the table. The side benches are covered with blue cushions. Sketchpads, notebooks, and a few books line the shelves. Two pots hang above a small stove in the kitchen area. A narrow door opens in to a small bathroom opposite the kitchen. Walking to the back of the boat, Lúcia enters the bedroom. Two more brass lamps are lit on each side of the bed. Crisp linen, a wool blanket. Lúcia lies down, she rests her head on the silky pillow and closes her eyes.

LÚCIA FEELS A GENTLE ROCKING, BACK AND FORTH. It is as though she were lying in a hammock at home in the shade of the ipê tree, her eyes closed, her mother rocking her soothingly.

She opens her eyes. The portholes cast a blinding light. She looks out: The sky. The sea. A deep, luminous blue sparkling with glitter. Lúcia climbs on deck. The ocean is immense, the sky is infinite, clear and open all around her. The sails are full. All is quiet. The squeaking ropes, the foam fizzing against the hull fill the silence with color. Turning to the prow, Lúcia can make out a thin line of a darker blue over the horizon: An island, or perhaps a cluster of islands.

As the sun sets, the ocean and sky turn pink, then purple, blending in the evening haze. Distant lights shimmer along the coastline. The relief sharpens: A rocky cliff, green hills, a

coconut grove. Past the cape, a long sandy beach glows in the moonlight. Anchored in the middle of a well-protected cove, a ship sparkles with a thousand lights.

Lúcia sees the people aboard the ship. A man and a woman turn toward her, smiling. They wave at her. As they call her name, she recognizes the sound of their voices.

A bell is ringing aboard the ship. And now more bells. Lúcia awakes. In the beds next to hers the other girls are still asleep. Brought in by the cool morning breeze, the ringing of bells fills the dormitory. Lúcia runs to the open window just in time to catch a glimpse of the herd of cows being led through the village.